Crystal Woods
Emma-Lucy Stories

A special message from Emma-Lucy Stories

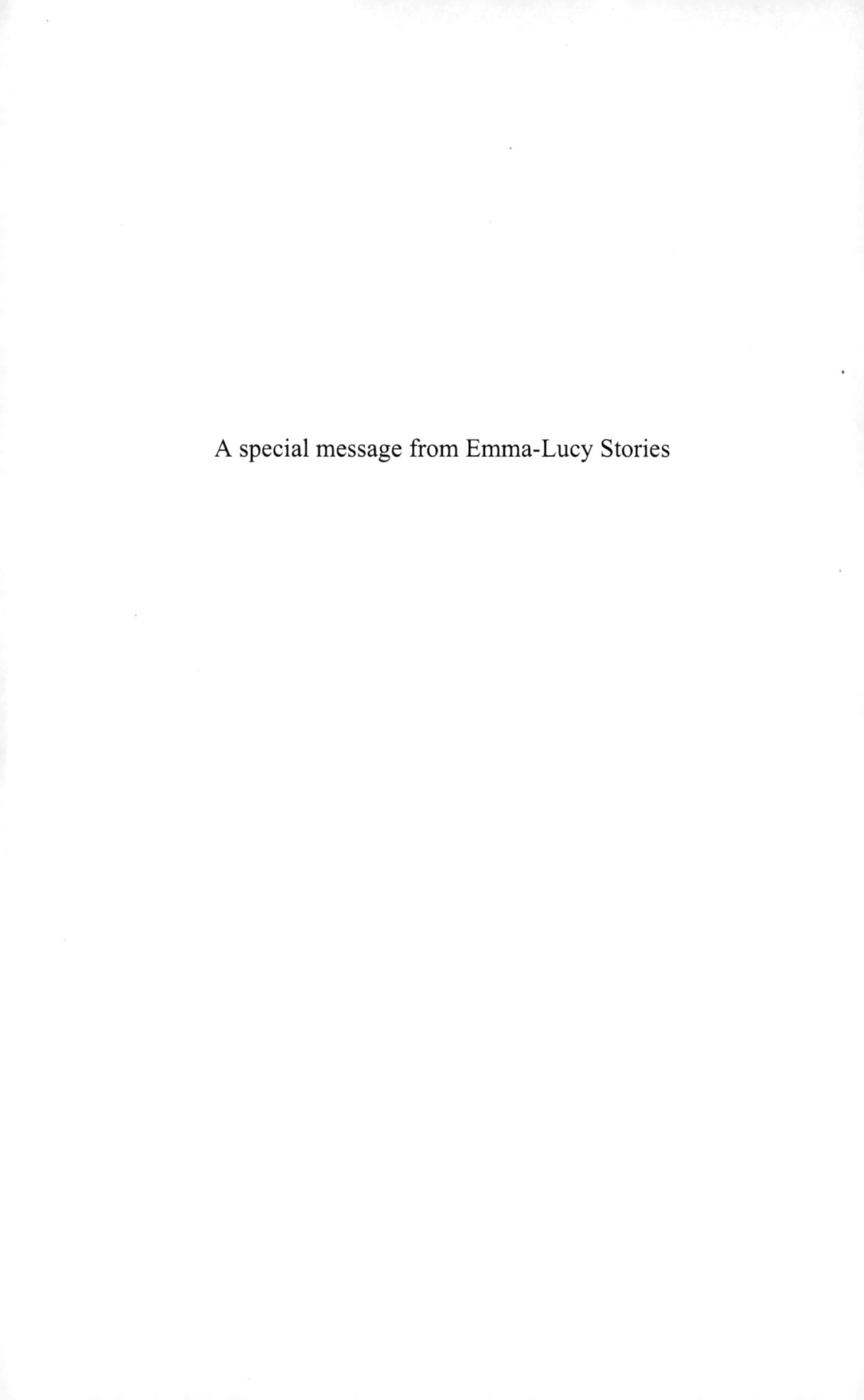

Contents

1. Who are you?
2. Returning
3. Reunion
4. Meetings
5. Secrets
6. The plan
7. Takeover
8. Saving Crystal Woods
9. Here comes Christmas
10. Zoe's choice

Chapter one – Who are you?

"Madison, darling. Could you come downstairs please?" shouted Mrs Nicholas up the stairs.

I, Madison-Rose rushed downstairs with my big sister Hannah.

Hannah was 19 years old, and the older of Madison-Rose and the eldest daughter of Sophie Elizabeth and Michael Nicholas. When she was Madison-Rose's age, her grandma (her mum's mum) forced her to
get rid of all her teddies and stopped collecting them. Her favourite teddy bear was a bear called Zoe who had two big black eyes and a big brown nose, two paws and feet. She had belonged to Sophie at first when Sophie was a little girl and her mum forced Sophie to get rid of her teddies (the same thing as what Elizabeth did to Hannah) and put Zoe into a box and into her attic but then she moved, and Zoe ended up in the boot of a Toyota and ended up in Japan

But then she got told by her mother, she has a half-brother and went on a search to find him and ended up in Crystal woods next to a camping site in Cornwall called St Meryl's and the forest was hidden. Inside the woods, there lived Harry (the boss) who was big and giant (he was yellow and wore a pink ribbon) Rosie and Josie (twin bears) Lily, Uni, Rainbow and Star (unicorns) Violet-Rose (she has white fur, red nose and two black eyes, Rory (a plainly peach fur and a dark peach nose) Chocolate (half-brother of Zoe, he's dark brown with light brown nose and black eyes) Rudolph who is the only reindeer in the forest (he's brown, and a red and white tiny nose and wore a red and white striped scarf) Ruby (he's light peach fur with tiny black eyes and a button brown nose) snowflake (white fur, red and green scarf and wore a pair of reindeer ears that were brown and had black eyes), Petals (she was another unicorn that lived there, she was white with a pink mare, pink ears, pink horn and big black eyes) cuddles (he was big but not as big as Harry, he was brown, had big black eyes, a big black nose and wore a red ribbon) Ginger (she is similar to Cuddles, but she had ginger coloured fur had a red heart on the bottom of one foot, a big black nose and two black eyes and a big smile) Magnificent (who is also a unicorn and the smallest one that lived there, she had dark pink fur, purple paws and feet and a sparkly light purple horn and black eyes) polar bear (light blue fur, black eyes and nose with white feet and paws) patches (she was orange, brown feet at the bottom, a brown button nose and black eyes) fudge Chocolate (all of her was brown, she had a dark brown nose and brown eyes) White chocolate (again he was all white but he had black eyes and nose)

I wonder what Madison-Rose is doing" said Rosie "yeah, I miss her, I wish she didn't have to go back to England," said Star "and Hannah, Star. But she had to go back, her family holiday ended" said Lily don't forget Hannah" said Rudolph their grandmother doesn't sound very nice, forcing Hannah not to collect teddy bears," said Fudge Chocolate.

Harry walked over; he was gigantic. He was the boss. He wore a pink ribbon and the rest of him was yellow and he had big black eyes. He was very soft.

He smiled at the animals.

Then some other animals began to walk over to them.

Harry smiled at them all nervously.

The blue teddy bear with black eyes and white paws smiled at them friendly.

"Hello" she said

The animals smiled but felt scared.

Harry smiled nervously.

"Hello, who are you?" he asked.

Chapter two – Returning

"What is it, mummy?" I asked.

Mrs Nicholas smiled at me and Hannah then Mr Nicholas came over.

"Mum? Come on, what is it?" asked Hannah.

Mr and Mrs Nicholas looked at each other grinning then looked at us.

"We are going on holiday," said Mrs Nicholas.

"No," said Hannah grinning "yes," said Mr Nicholas smiling at his daughter.

"Daddy, this is a joke isn't it?" I asked "no, it's not sweetheart. I'm being genuinely serious. We are going on holiday" said Mr Nicholas sounding serious.

"Oh, my Christmas, where?" I asked jumping up and down screaming with joy "Cornwall, St Meryl's. Where we stayed last Christmas", said Mr Nicholas smiling.

My sister and I looked at each other.

We knew what that meant. We could see Zoe and all our new friends again.

"Steven and Jade are coming with us" said Mrs Nicholas.

We both stared at our mum. Over the summer, Jade and Steven have become very close to me and they are like part of our family.

No way" said Hannah "oh mum, dad. We love you" said Hannah hugging mum and dad.

"Let's go pack Maddy," said Hannah "when do you know when we leave?" asked Hannah "first thing tomorrow. We are picking Steven and Jade up" said Mr Nicholas "okay dad, let's go pack Maddy," said Hannah and started walking upstairs. I started to follow my sister then stopped.

"Daddy?" I asked, "yes princess?" asked Mr Nicholas "I have a question," I said, "what is that sweetie?" asked Mr Nicholas now laughing because he had an idea what the question was. "How many teddys can I bring?" I asked.

Mr and Mrs Nicholas and Hannah laughed, and my dad smiled at me as he was right about the question and he wasn't surprised.

"As many as you want honey," said Mrs Nicholas "okay mummy, let's go quick," I said rushing upstairs and pulled Hannah along with me.

We reached our bedroom. It had two single beds, bookcases, a computer desk that Hannah's laptop was kept, pictures of Hannah's friend Jade, pictures of her and her boyfriend Steven and our family including pictures of Hannah and me. It was also surrounded by suffered animals.

"Maddy?" asked Hannah "what if Zoe isn't there in Crystal Woods or if we can't find it?" asked Hannah.

"Hannah-Banana?" I asked "yes Maddy," asked Hannah "I love you," I said.

This was the first time I had said I love you to Hannah since we had made up. We hadn't said it since I was 4 years old.

Hannah looked at me very confused.

"You haven't said I love you to me since you were 4 years old?" asked Hannah smiling giving me a hug "Maddy, I love you so much, I really do. What teddys are you going to take with us?" asked Hannah.

I looked at her then looked around our room thinking.

"I am taking 4 teddy bears," I said confident "okay, what are their names?" asked Hannah "Jasmine," I said, and I held up a small unicorn, that was a jellycat and she was light pink and had a dark pink mare. Hannah smiled at me.

Then I held up a green monster with one big white eye.

"OMG, isn't he from that Disney movie? What's it called?" asked Hannah trying to think.

"He's Mike from Monsters, Inc Han," I said "that's it, who got you that?" asked Hannah "you did, you muppet. You and Steven for my birthday" I said.

Hannah looked confused for a couple of minutes then suddenly remembered.

"Oh yes, I remember," said Hannah.

"So, what other ones are you bringing?" asked Hannah.

I held up a bear that was yellow, had big black eyes wearing a red bow then I held up a cat wearing a unicorn costume. She had ginger and white fur with a tiny pink button nose.

I smiled at my sister as I put my teddys into my suitcase and zipped it up. I had packed clothes and bath stuff. Not just teddys.

"Their names are Alexander and Button Nose," I said.

Hannah smiled as she too zipped her suitcase up.

"Girls?" shouted Mr Nicholas from the bottom of the stairs.

We came downstairs hand in hand.

"We've done daddy," I said.

Mr Nicholas smiled as we both handed him our suitcases.

He struggled to left mine.

"Maddison, darling what on earth do you have in there. A pair of bricks?" he asked laughing.

"What time are we setting off dad?" asked Hannah.

"7:30 am," said Mr Nicholas now winking.

Hannah was not the best for waking up.

"Okay, we'll head off to bed then. We'll see you tomorrow morning" said Hannah.

Mr Nicholas looked surprised.

"Night mummy and daddy," I said kissing both of them on the check.

Mr and Mrs Nicholas watched and smiled.

"Michael, tell me the truth. What time are we actually set off?" asked Mrs Nicholas.

"Darling, I don't know what you mean," said Mr Nicholas. Mrs Nicholas looked at him seriously

Mr Nicholas knew he was caught out.

"Okay fine, 2 pm," said Michael truthfully laughing.

Mrs Nicholas hit his arm then joined in laughing.

"You're mean," she said in between laughing.

We got to our bedroom and started getting ready for bed.

"Hannah?" I asked as we got into our beds.

"Yes, Mads, what is it?" asked Hannah "I love you," I said.

I had already said this, but Hannah smiled.

"I love you so much Maddy, you are one amazing little girl," said Hannah. I smiled blushing.

The next morning, Mr Nicholas got our suitcases into the car along with all the camping equipment when I, Hannah and my mum got ourselves ready.

An hour later, we were all ready to go.

"You ready girls?" asked Mr Nicholas as Jade got into the car.

"Yes, let's get Steven," said Hannah.

"Hannah, darling. Don't get angry" said Mr Nicholas "why? What's wrong?" asked Hannah we weren't going to leave until 2 PM, your father thought it'd be funny to trick you that we need to leave early," said Mrs Nicholas.

"DAD. How could you?" asked Hannah laughing "mum, it is kind of funny though," said Hannah.

When we got to Steven's house. Hannah hopped out the car.

Hannah knocked on the front door.

Steven's mother Paige answered, "hey Hannah, you alright love?" asked Miss Potter.

"Yes, I'm good thank you, Miss Potter," said Hannah and smiled as we saw Steven.

"Okay, have you got everything?" asked Miss Potter "yes, mum," said Steven rolling his eyes but smiled. His mum kissed him "okay, stay safe both of you. Text me when you get there. Love you" said Miss Potter.

"Love you more mum, we will," said Steven waving as they headed to the car. Miss Potter shut the door behind her and went back to her knitting.

Hannah and Steven got into the car next to each other.

Mr Nicholas looked in the mirror looking at Steven.

"Alright, lad?" asked Mr Nicholas "I'm good to thank you, Mr Nicholas," said Steven "thank you for inviting me" he added "son, please call us Sophie and Michael," said Mrs Nicholas.

Steven smiled.

"Right, are you all ready?" asked Mr Nicholas.

"Yes," we all said back.

"Oh yeah Steven, we weren't going to leave until 2 PM," said Hannah.

With a shocked look on his face, we were on our way to Cornwall.

Chapter three – Reunited

When we got to St Meryl's in Cornwall.

We all got out of the car.

"Mummy, daddy, can I go for a walk?" I asked.

Mr and Mrs Nicholas looked at each other than at me.

"Yes, of course, you can darling. Han, can you go with her please sweetheart?" asked Mrs Nicholas.

Hannah looked at our parents.

"Of course, do you want help setting the tent up?" asked Hannah.

Steven looked at Hannah.

"I can do it, babe, don't worry," said Steven.

Hannah smiled at Steven "Jade? Do you fancy coming?" asked Hannah.

"Yes," said Jade.

"We'll see you guys later then," said Mr Nicholas starting to get the camping gear out of the car "be safe, love you" he added.

"I love you too daddy," I said.

We all waved as we held each other's hands. Hannah in the middle and me and Jade on each end and wandered into the woods.

As we walked into the woods. We could see loads of trees although it was all covered in snow.

Rosie, Josie, Lily and Harry all came over to us.

I smiled at them then I looked around confused.

The friends looked at me.

"What's wrong Maddy?" asked Josie.

"Where's Zoe?" I asked.

"We don't know but it's so good to see you. We thought we'd never see you again" said Harry.

We all laughed then gave each other a hug.

"I hope Zoe is okay," I said.

Chocolate, Zoe's half-brother came skipping over.

Then he saw us.

"Maddy! You're back" he cried and hugged me.

"Chocolate, we are just wondering where Zoe is?" I asked as soon as I said this.

Zoe, light brown fur, a big dark nose with two black eyes came over with a bear that we'd never seen before.

She was all dark brown fur with two black eyes and an even darker brown nose.

We smiled as they came over.

"Zoe!" I cried hugging Zoe.

"Who is that?" asked Lily.

Chocolate came over to us.

"This is my, I mean our cousin Fudge Chocolate," said Zoe.

Chapter four – Fudge Chocolate

We all looked at Zoe and the other bear confused.

Who was she?

I smiled and handed out my hand, but the bear stepped back looking scared.

"Fudge, these are my friends. It's okay" said Zoe "but they're humans," said Fudge "yeah but they're believers Fudge," said Chocolate "it's okay!" said Zoe and smiled at Fudge. Fudge smiled back and then stepped towards me.

I handed out my hand for her to shake it.

I smiled.

"I'm pleased to meet you. Did you know that you were Zoe and Chocolate's cousin?" I asked, "not until Zoe told me when she found me on the side of the road," said Fudge.

We all smiled back just then a white bear came over who looked a lot like Fudge Chocolate.

She smiled.

"Hello," she said, "who are you?" asked Fudge.

"My name is White Chocolate," he said.

Fudge looked at him.

"My name is Fudge Chocolate," said Fudge shocked.

"So, you both have Chocolate as your surname?" asked Zoe.

"Yes, weirdly," said Fudge Chocolate "and you look the same?" I asked "yes," said both White and Fudge Chocolate.

They looked at us now confused.

"What is it?" asked White Chocolate.

They all looked at me then we looked at Hannah.

"Are you thinking the same as me?" asked Hannah.

We all nodded.

Hannah looked at Fudge and White Chocolate.

"I think you might be brother and sister which makes you both Zoe and Chocolate's cousins," said Hannah.

Fudge and White Chocolate looked at us than each other and us again.

"I think you might be twin bears like Rosie and Josie who also live here," said Hannah.

Again, Fudge and White Chocolate looked at each other than at us completely in shock

Chapter five – Secrets

"Didn't you know that you were twins?" I asked.

The twin bears looked at us then at each other.

Back at the campsite, Michael and Sophie had an unexpected visitor.

Sophie's mother Elizabeth. But why is she here and alone? Where's Jimmy?

"Mum? What are you doing here? Where's dad?" asked Sophie shocked to see her mother "I've come to see you, Sophie. Dad is at home" said Elizabeth.

Back in Crystal Woods, Chocolate had gone off somewhere.

"Hope Chocolate is okay. I wonder who the call was from" said Zoe.

"But why didn't we know we were twins?" asked White Chocolate "I don't know, perhaps you got separated" I said. Chocolate had gone further into the woods.

"Mother? Are you there?" he asked "yes, I'm here," said the person on the other end of the phone.

"Why are you calling me?" asked Chocolate "did you and Zoe manage to find each other?" asked the mother of Chocolate "yes, we bumped into each other in London but why didn't you tell us we were related? And what about Fudge and White Chocolate?" asked Chocolate.

The mother signed.

Back at the campsite, Sophie, Michael and Elizabeth stared at each other.

"Where are the girls?" asked Elizabeth "off playing hide and seek, you know that Maddy has brought some teddys with her," said Sophie beaming.

Elizabeth, however, wasn't impressed and rolled her eyes.

"Aren't they a bit too old to play hide and seek?" asked Elizabeth.
Michael signed.

"They are not too old and if you don't like how WE raise our daughters then you can go back home. We didn't ask you to come" said Michael.

Elizabeth raised her eyebrows "don't talk to me like that" said Elizabeth "they are too old to play silly games like hide and seek or believe teddy bears are real. God, Sophie, when you were that age, you didn't believe in teddy bears" said Elizabeth "that's because you didn't let me believe that they are real mum. You took my most precious bear out of them and stuffed her into a box and put her into a box and you did the exactly the same to Hannah when she was that age and when you recognised Zoe, you took her away from Hannah and forced her not to believe in teddy bears which affected her relationship with Maddy. I don't know how it happened, but they have got closer again and they are inseparable" said Sophie "aren't they?" she asked Michael.

He nodded his head.

"Sophie, I don't understand. You had a great childhood. I was only trying to do the right thing" said Elizabeth

Chapter six – Take over

"What do you mean I wrecked your childhood?" asked Elizabeth "you took the one thing I loved the most away from me and forced me to get rid of all of my other teddy bears and to not believe in them anymore," said Sophie.

Back in Crystal Woods, Chocolate walked towards us and then some other bear, a sheep, a kangaroo and a giraffe came over.

They walked up to us, we all looked confused.

"Who are you?" I asked, "I'm Charlie" said one of the bears "I'm Mo" said the kangaroo "I'm Cotton socks" said the sheep "and I'm George" said the giraffe "what are you doing here?" asked Zoe.

"We want to take over this forest, I mean woods" said Cotton socks.

"What do you mean, take over?" asked Chocolate "humans are here" said Charlie.

"and they shouldn't be. Humans don't believe in us anymore. So, you need to go" said Cotton socks "why do you want to live here? We live here" said Zoe "because humans shouldn't be allowed to come into this part of the campsite. It's all about their phones and their computers these days. They don't believe in us anymore like they used to" they all said.

We all looked at them but headed out of the part of the woods.

"What are you going to do?" I asked "give up, it's their choice to live there then we should respect it" said Chocolate.

Chocolate walked off and we watched him in the distance confused "is chocolate okay?" I asked "I don't know, he's been acting strange recently" said Zoe. When some other bears came over.

Compared to Charlie and his friends, they seem happier.

"Oh gosh, more bears! At last," said one of them then spotted me, Hannah, Jade and Steven.

They smiled at us.

One of them politely offered one of their paws.

She was all purple that wore a dress that I recognized as the dress that the main character Dorothy Gale wore in the 1939 wizards of oz movie.

"Hey," she said friendly and smiling.

"Hello" said Zoe smiling back at the bear "who are you?" asked Lily "I'm Eloise but everyone calls me El," said Eloise smiling.

"I'm Zoe, this is Lily, Harry, Uni, Rainbow, Harry, Rudolph, my half-brother Chocolate who isn't here right now, he is acting strange and we are wondering why because it's not like him, this is Rory, White and Chocolate Fudge who are twins and my cousins. Welcome to Crystal Woods, it's been taken over" said Zoe.

"By whom? Can I help?" asked Eloise "by some bear Charlie, a kangaroo Mo, a baby sheep Cotton socks and a giraffe called George. They want us gone especially Maddy, her sister and their friends because they don't think humans should be allowed here" said Zoe "but I have a plan" she said.

Chapter seven – the plan

"So, what's your plan?" asked Uni "make posters and refuse to leave Crystal Woods," said Zoe.

We all smiled at Zoe, but Chocolate looked away.

"There's no point saving Crystal Woods" said Chocolate.

We all looked at him confused and he walked off.

"What was that about?" I asked "I don't know but I am worried about him. He's been acting strange since he had that mystery phone call" said Zoe.

I smiled "maybe Lily should go and see if he's okay and find out what's wrong? While we make these posters", said Harry looking at Lily.

She smiled at us and went to go and find Chocolate while we started these posters.

Lily wondered further into the woods and spotted Chocolate.

"Hey Choco, what's up? We're all worried about you" said Lily.

Chocolate signed.

Back at where we were in the part of the woods, we nearly finished the posters.

Lily wondered further into the woods and spotted Chocolate.

"Hey Choco, what's up? We're all worried about you" said Lily.

Chocolate signed as he looked at Lily.

Back at where we were in the woods, we had nearly finished all the posters.

I held my poster up to show everyone

It read ...

SAVE CRYSTAL WOODS!

Save our home

"Oh Maddy, I love it" said Zoe.

All my friends smiled.

Charlie and his friends came over.

Further in the woods, Lily was looking at Chocolate.

He looked at her.

"What's going on Chocolate?" she asked.

He signed.

"Okay, the reason why I am acting strange is because you know I had a phone call the other day" said Chocolate "yes" said Lily.

"Well it was from our mother; she's been talking to me and she has invited me and Zoe back to Japan and I have no idea how to tell Zoe" said Chocolate.

Back in the main part of the woods.

"We are not moving, this is our home and you can't take over and force us to leave Crystal Woods," said Zoe "Madison-Rose has always believed that there is another world and so did Hannah when she was Madison-Rose's age, she believed in teddy bears and a big collector but their grandmother took me from her, put me into their attic in a box but I managed to climb down the ladder and outside and ended up in an old abandoned Toyota car and came to London. Anyway, their grandmother forced Hannah to get rid of all her teddy bears, not to believe in them anymore and this affected her relationship with Maddy because she got very jealous about Maddy's collection but she didn't believe we existed because of her grandmother until she came to St Meryl's and Maddy got lost while playing hide and seek with Hannah and Hannah was asked to go and look for her sister and that is when Hannah started to believe that we are real Charlie and that Maddy and Hannah's relationship got better. You can still live here but this is our home" said Zoe.

Chapter eight – Saving Crystal Woods

Charlie looked at Zoe and all of us.

Further, in the woods, Lily was looking at Chocolate worried.

What are you going to do?" asked Lily "I really don't know Lil. part of me wants to return to Japan so I am with my mum obviously, but I would miss you guys too" said Chocolate.

Back in the main part of the woods.

Charlie and his friends were still looking at all the bears.

Hannah, Jade, Steven and I, however, had gone to the campsite, St Meryl's that was right next door to Crystal Woods.

We walked over to my parents and spotted grandma Elizabeth.

Both Hannah and I don't really like our grandmother.

We smiled as we walked over to them.

Mrs Nicholas smiled back.

"There you are, you've been gone a long time" said Mrs Nicholas "did you have fun playing hide and seek?" she asked.

I looked at my sister and our friends panicked then looked at my mum and dad.

"Yes, it was really fun. Nan, what are you doing here?" I asked looking at my grandmother.

Back in Crystal Woods, further in the woods Chocolate still looking at Lily.

"What would you do?" asked Chocolate "I know what you could do" said Lily grinning "what's that?" asked Chocolate smiling back at Lily "seeing as you would like to go back to Japan to be with your mother which I totally get because I miss my mum terribly. You could go to Japan with Zoe for a holiday as you will miss us as much as we will miss you" said Lily.

Back in the main part of the woods, Charlie looked at Zoe.

"Zoe, we don't want you to leave Crystal Woods. I am sorry that we were trying to take over your home" said Charlie smiling at Zoe and Zoe smiled back.

Further in the woods, it began to snow.

"Hey, it's snowing" said Lily and Lily and Chocolate started walking back to the main part of the woods paw in hove.

In St Meryl's Elizabeth looked at us.

"Where's Grandad?" asked Hannah.

"Hannah, you are 17 years old. You're too old for play hide and seek and Madison, you're nearly 10 years old. You need to stop believing in teddy bears" said Grandma Elizabeth.

"Mum, stop. Don't do this" said Mrs Nicholas furious.

Back in Crystal Woods, Chocolate and Lily came over.

"Oh goodness, Chocolate there you are! Are you okay?" asked Zoe "yes, I'm sorry" said Chocolate. Zoe smiled.

"Is Crystal Woods saved?" asked Lily smiling.

"Yes! Charlie and his friends are going to be living with us in Crystal Woods. You can thank Maddy, Hannah and their friends" said Zoe "why?" asked Chocolate "because they are the reason Charlie reconsider about throwing us out of Crystal Woods. Because Charlie and his friends thought that no human believes in us anymore, it's about their phones and computers now but Maddy and Hannah believe in us and they always have" said Zoe smiling.

All the bears smiled at Zoe.

Back at St Meryl's, Elizabeth looked at our mum and us.

"Sophie, they are both too old to play hide and seek or even believe that teddy bears are real," said Grandma Elizabeth. Sophie looked at her mum disgusted "No. Don't do the same thing to them that you did to me" said Sophie as the snow started to fall...

Chapter nine – Here comes Christmas

As snow fell heavily, Elizabeth looked at her daughter and granddaughters unimpressed and raised her eyebrows.

"Why don't you want to say it Sophie?" asked grandma Elizabeth.

Back in the woods of Crystal Woods.

"I've just had an idea," said Zoe "what is that?" asked Josie "did you know that Christmas is soon," said Zoe "what's that?" asked Star, "Maddy told me it is an annual festive commentary the birth of Jesus Christ," said Zoe "okay and what is your idea?" asked Uni "do a little Christmas party for Maddy, Hannah and their friends before they have to go home," said Zoe.

Back in St Meryl's, Sophie looked at Grandma Elizabeth.

"Mum, they are not too old for hiding and seek or believing in teddy bears. Don't do the same thing you did to them, and what you did to Hannah when she was younger but it didn't work. They're not your kids" said Sophie.

Elizabeth looked at Sophie.

"Okay, maybe I was wrong for what I did when you were little, forcing you not to believe in teddy bears and doing the same to Hannah and now Maddy," said Elizabeth "I'm sorry Sophie, I really am. I thought I was doing the right thing taking Zoe away from you" she added hugging Sophie.

Back in Crystal woods, Zoe and her furry friends had nearly finished the Christmas dinner for Maddy when Maddy and friends came over to the bears.

What's this?" I asked looking around the woods.

"Christmas has come to Crystal Woods," said Harry grinning.

I stared at my fury friends.

Lily looked at Chocolate panicking "I think you should tell her choc" said Lily.

Zoe looked at Chocolate looking confused.

"Tell me what? What's going on?" asked Zoe,

"Okay, you know I had a phone call?" asked Chocolate "yes," said Zoe "it was our mum, she's invited us to go back to Japan," said Chocolate.

Chapter ten – Zoe's choice

"What do you mean?" asked Zoe "she wants us to come home Zoe," said Chocolate.

I looked at Zoe and Chocolate with my friends and my sister.

"Wait but I don't want you to go. We've only just been able to save Crystal Woods from being taken over" said Lily "yeah same, we've only just been able to find each other" said White Chocolate "and thanks to Fudge Chocolate of course" he added quickly smiling at his twin.

Zoe looked turned, looking at her brother, her friends then at us.

"Maddy, can I have a word please?" asked Zoe I nodded, and Hannah and I followed Zos and we stopped and stood by a tree.

"What do you think I should do?" asked Zoe I obviously don't want you to go but it's a chance to be reunited with your mother," I said "I agree," said, Hannah.

Zoe smiled at both of us.

"it's been great meeting you Madison and being with, you again Hannah. Thank you so much for all help saving our home" said Zoe hugging me and Hannah.

Hannah smiled at me

"That was really brave Maddy, I'm really proud of you," said Hannah and I smiled at my sister.

Zoe walked back over to her furry friends while Jade and Steven came over to us,

"Everything okay?" asked Steven "no, we might never see Zoe again," said Hannah.

Jade and Steven signed.

"She's decided to go back to Japan with Chocolate," said Hannah "why?" asked Jade "to be reunited with her mother," I said.

Jade and Steven hugged me and Hannah as we started crying.

Zoe came over to us smiling.

"Can you please come with me?" asked Zoe.

Hannah and I wiped our tears away and we followed Zoe along with Steven and Jade.

Snow started to fall heavily again, and we reached the table that had the tablecloth with plates, knives, forks and Christmas crackers.

What's this?" I asked, "Christmas has come to Crystal Woods," said Zoe smiling.

We all smiled back, and we all sat down. I sat next to Lily and Rosie, Hannah sat down to Uni and Rainbow, Jade sat down to Zoe and Chocolate and Steven sat down to Josie and Fudge Chocolate and we all tucked in.

Printed in Great Britain
by Amazon